# Lucy the Magnificent

DAMIAN MORGAN

Illustrated by Rae Dale

sundance™ Newbridge®

# The Characters

Lucy

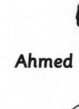
Ahmed

Mrs. Snowden

Mr. Assad

2

# The Story Setting

# TABLE OF CONTENTS

**Chapter 1**
An Unofficial Opening .. 6

**Chapter 2**
Searching . . . . . . . . . . . . . 18

**Chapter 3**
The Thief Escapes . . . . . . 30

**Chapter 4**
Just in Time . . . . . . . . . . . 48

**Chapter 5**
The Opening . . . . . . . . . . 54

# CHAPTER 1

## An Unofficial Opening

Ahmed found Lucy in the staff room of his father's art gallery. He was excited.

"Your mom's show is ready. Let's sneak a peek," he said with a grin.

"Your father will be angry if we look before the official opening," said Lucy.

"We'll use the side door. He won't know!"

Just then, Mrs. Williams, the cleaning lady, shuffled in. She was in a bad mood.

"Hi Mrs. Williams. Did you finish the Blue Room?" Ahmed asked.

Mrs. Williams took the vacuum cleaner out of the closet. "Is a cleaner ever finished?" she sighed loudly. "Huh! I haven't even started the vacuuming."

"But you'll clean the Blue Room first, won't you?" Ahmed asked. "Lucy's mom will be a star when the show opens."

Mrs. Williams stomped out of the room.

"Mrs. Williams isn't usually so grumpy. I wonder what's wrong," said Ahmed.

"Watch this," Lucy said. She put a coin on the table and covered it with a cup. She put three more cups next to it. "Which cup hides the coin?" she asked.

Ahmed pointed to the right cup.

"OK. Now, watch carefully." Lucy quickly moved the cups around. "Where's the coin now?"

Ahmed pointed. Lucy lifted the cup. There was no coin. Ahmed stared. "How did you do that?"

"It's because I'm Lucy the Magnificent!"

Lucy picked up a cup. There was the coin.

Ahmed grinned. "Cool! Now do you want to see your mother's show?"

They walked down the hall, and Ahmed unlocked the side door into the Blue Room. Lucy gasped.

At home, her mother's paintings were usually stacked against the walls. Lucy had never paid much attention to them. Now they hung on bare walls, and spotlights made them gleam.

Lucy stared at the portraits of singers, sports stars, and ordinary people. For the first time, she realized how talented her mother was.

Lucy's mom had been asked to paint the official portrait of the President of the United States. The painting hung on the far wall of the gallery under a blue velvet curtain. In half an hour, the President himself was going to open the art show and unveil his portrait.

Ahmed said, "I Ahmed Assad, President of the United States, declare this art show open!" He pulled a cord and the curtain opened to reveal an empty picture frame.

Lucy gasped, "Ahmed! Someone has stolen the painting!"

# CHAPTER 2

## Searching

Ahmed looked in horror at the empty frame. "This is terrible! Who could have stolen the painting?"

Lucy said, "There must be a burglar alarm. Where is it?"

Lucy saw the alarm and ran toward it.

"No, don't!" Ahmed shouted.

Lucy stopped. "Why not?"

"If we pull the alarm, the security doors will close and lock. The opening of the show will be delayed. The President will be here soon. Tomorrow he's leaving the country. If he doesn't open the show today, he won't be able to do it at all."

"What should we do?" asked Lucy.

"We have to find the thief," said Ahmed.

Lucy stared at the empty frame. "How?"

"We'll ask Mr. Miller, the guard, if he's
seen anyone suspicious," said Ahmed.

In the hall, Lucy stopped. "There are only two doors into the Blue Room, right?"

Ahmed nodded. "Mr. Miller guards the main doors. Mrs. Williams used the side door. How about if I ask Mrs. Williams and you ask Mr. Miller?"

"OK," said Lucy.

Lucy walked into the reception room.
Long tables were covered with platters of
food. A dozen guests had already arrived.

Lucy hurried over toward Mr. Miller.
A hand on her shoulder stopped her.

"Lucy!" It was her mother. "Slow down. The photographer wants to take some photos of us with the President. So don't go anywhere."

"OK, Mom." Lucy tried to keep walking, but her mother stopped her again.

"Why don't you stay here with me? There isn't long to wait until the opening."

"OK, Mom. I just have to do one thing."

Ahmed's father came over. "Mrs. Snowden, there's someone I'd like you to meet."

Lucy darted over toward Mr. Miller. His pencil-thin moustache quivered in a smile when he saw Lucy.

"Are you excited about the opening?" he asked. "Your mother sure is!"

Lucy whispered, "Has anyone been inside the Blue Room today?"

"Just your mom and Mr. Assad. Then I locked the door. Look." He rattled the doorknob. "Is something wrong?"

"No." Lucy stepped backward. She avoided her mother and left the room.

Lucy checked the staff room. It was
empty, but as she was leaving, she heard
a noise. She stepped back into the room.
The noise was coming from the closet.

Lucy opened the closet door, and there was Ahmed! His mouth was covered with a cloth. His hands and feet were tied with an electrical cord.

# CHAPTER 3

## The Thief Escapes

Lucy untied the cloth from Ahmed's face.

Ahmed said, "I asked Mrs. Williams about the painting. She pushed me to the floor, tied me up, and shoved me in here!"

Lucy said, "I didn't see her in the hall."

"She has the painting!" said Ahmed.
"She rolled up the canvas and slid it into
a piece of tube from the vacuum cleaner.
We have to find her."

"Where? Where should we look?"

"She parks her car behind the building."
Ahmed headed for the door. "Come on!"

Lucy reached into the closet and grabbed
two more segments of vacuum cleaner
tube. Then she raced after Ahmed.

The art gallery was in the front of an old warehouse. The back of the warehouse was divided into storerooms and artists' studios.

Ahmed stopped. "Mrs. Williams could be hiding in any of these rooms."

"No, she'll want to get away fast."

"You're right. I'll look for her car. You check some of the rooms, just to be sure," said Ahmed.

"OK." Lucy glanced into the first studio and saw a purple coat. "Ahmed, come back!" she shouted. "Look in here. There's Mrs. Williams's coat."

At the back of the studio was a door. Lucy opened it and gasped. There was Mrs. Williams, tied to a chair with a towel over her mouth. Lucy dropped the tubes and removed the towel.

Mrs. Williams said, "I'm sorry, Ahmed. Jim Speers forced me to take the painting. He said that if I didn't, he'd make it look like I was not doing my job, and he'd get me fired. I know it was wrong. But I need this job, so I did it."

Lucy said, "Who's Jim Speers?"

Ahmed said, "This is his studio, but he hasn't paid his rent for six months. Do you know where he went, Mrs. Williams?"

She looked up. "He stole my car keys."

Lucy said, "He must be gone by now."

"Maybe not," said Ahmed. "He stopped to tie up Mrs. Williams. Come on!"

Lucy grabbed the pipes and raced after Ahmed. At the back of the warehouse was a large garage door. It opened onto a loading dock where trucks made deliveries. The door was slowly creaking up from the floor. A short man stood by it, waiting for it to open.

Lucy whispered, "Is that him?"

"Yes," said Ahmed.

Lucy pointed. "Look, there's the tube!"

Ahmed started to tiptoe across the floor.

Jim Speers turned. "Hey!" He shook his fists. "You kids stay back."

Lucy said, "You can't take my mom's painting!"

Ahmed said, "That's the President's official portrait!"

"And someone will pay a lot to get it back," Jim said.

Lucy dropped the two tubes next to
the one holding the painting.

"Hey! Leave that!" yelled Jim.

Lucy took two tubes and changed their
positions twice. Jim pushed Lucy
backward.

Jim grabbed a tube. "You can't fool me."

Ahmed rushed forward, but Jim pushed him onto the dusty floor.

Jim stepped outside and waved the pipe at them. "When I sell this, I'll be able to buy my own studio!"

# CHAPTER 4

## Just in Time

Lucy stood up. Her new clothes were covered in dust.

"We'd better get Mr. Miller to call the police," Ahmed said.

Lucy grabbed the pipes and followed. "How long before the opening?"

Ahmed glanced at his watch. "Only ten minutes," he groaned.

As they ran, they passed Mrs. Williams in the studio. She looked worried. "Did you find Jim Speers?" she asked.

"Don't worry, he's gone," Lucy said. "Excuse us, but we have to hurry."

When they reached the Blue Room, Lucy pointed toward the side door of the Blue Room. "Unlock it for me, Ahmed."

"Why?"

"Just do it, Ahmed. Hurry!"

Ahmed hesitated.

"Ahmed!"

"I have to tell Mr. Miller!" he said, but he unlocked the door.

"Come in here. I'll need your help."

"What do you mean?" asked Ahmed.

Lucy threw Ahmed one of the pipes. He looked inside. It looked empty. Grinning, Lucy reached in the other pipe and pulled out the painting.

Ahmed gaped at her. "How did . . . ?"

"Remember, I'm Lucy the Magnificent!"
She turned to the frame. "I can't do a
perfect job, but it will be good enough."

Ahmed said, "So Jim Speers took . . ."

"An empty pipe. Hurry up and help me!"

# CHAPTER 5

## The Opening

Lucy reframed the painting and, with Ahmed's help, hung it on the wall. They stepped back to see if it was hanging straight.

"It looks good," Lucy said.

"Great! Now let's get out of here!"

Just then, they heard a key in the lock
of the main gallery doors.

Ahmed said, "Wait! The curtain!"

The blue curtain was open. Ahmed sped to the wall and yanked the curtain over the painting. They ran out the side door.

Lucy closed the door just as the gallery doors swung open and the President walked in.

Lucy and Ahmed joined the crowd
waiting to enter the Blue Room.

"Lucy! Where have you been? Look at
you. You can't have your photo taken
looking like that!" Lucy's mother glared
at Ahmed as she dragged Lucy away.

Ahmed followed the Snowdens into the gallery. He wanted to explain to Lucy's mother why Lucy was dirty, but the President was giving a speech. Then he opened the curtain, unveiling his portrait. Everyone clapped and cheered.

Ahmed searched the crowd, looking for
Lucy. He found her with the President
beside a table. On it were four cups.

"Which cup?" Lucy asked.

The President lifted a cup. "Oh."

There was nothing under the cup.
Lucy lifted another cup to reveal a coin.
"Lucy the Magnificent does it again!"

# GLOSSARY

**canvas**

a type of material
on which a picture
is painted

**gallery**

a place where artwork
is exhibited

**gleam**

to shine in the light

**reveal**

to make known

**segments**

separate sections

**unveil**

to remove a covering

# Talking with the Author and the Illustrator

## Damian Morgan (author)

*If there were only two colors in the world, what should they be?*
Black and white. Black and white television was just fine in the days when we didn't know about color television.

*Which animal would you most like to be?*
A Tasmanian tiger. Then at least the species wouldn't be extinct.

## Rae Dale (illustrator)

*What did you want to be when you grew up?*
A triceratops.

*What's your favorite game?*
Shopping.

**sundance** Newbridge®

Copyright © 2003 Sundance Newbridge Publishing

Published by Sundance Newbridge Publishing
33 Boston Post Road West, Suite 440, Marlborough, MA 01752
800-343-8204
*SundanceNewbridge.com*

Copyright © text Damian Morgan
Copyright © illustrations Rae Dale

First published 2000 as Sparklers by
Blake Education, Locked Bag 2022, Glebe 2037, Australia
Exclusive United States Distribution: Sundance Newbridge Publishing

ISBN: 978-0-7608-6972-7

Printed by Nordica International Ltd.
Manufactured in Guangzhou, China
February, 2019
Nordica Job#: CA21900141
SunNew PO#: 229216